William and Grandpa

BY ALICE SCHERTLE
ILLUSTRATIONS BY LYDIA DABCOVICH

LOTHROP, LEE & SHEPARD BOOKS · NEW YORK

For all grandpas
— A. S.

First Edition 1 2 3 4 5 6 7 8 9 10

Library of Congress Cataloging in Publication Data
Schertle, Alice. William and Grandpa.
Summary: William and Grandpa enjoy doing the things Grandpa did when he was a little boy, such as
trying to jump on their shadows, watching the stars from the roof of the house, and drinking hot chocolate.
[1. Grandfathers—Fiction] I. Dabcovich, Lydia, ill. II. Title. PZ7.S3442Wi 1989 [Fic] 88-666
ISBN 0-688-07580-0 ISBN 0-688-07581-9 (lib. bdg.)

The big yellow bus pulled into the station. William had a fluttery feeling in his stomach. What if Grandpa wasn't there to meet him?

Hissssssssss went the brakes, and William and the other passengers stood up and crowded into the aisle.

Bump! Bump! Bump! William pulled his duffel bag down the steep metal steps and stood on the station platform, trying to see over the heads of people hurrying past.

There was Grandpa, laughing and wrapping
William in a big bear hug. He picked up the duffel
and took William's hand, and off they went
together.

"You've been busy growing," Grandpa said.

William looked up at tall, white-haired Grandpa with his long white mustache and eyebrows that curled right up over his forehead. Grandpa's hand felt big and rough and warm. It made William feel safe and happy. "I learned a new song at school," said William. "It goes like this:

> I went to the animal fair,
> The birds and the beasts were there..."

Grandpa's gruff voice chimed in,

> "The big baboon
> By the light of the moon
> Was combing his auburn hair."

Down the street they went, singing away, and swinging their arms, and marching along to the music.

Grandpa squeezed William's hand. "That's not a new song, but I haven't thought of it since I was a boy."

William measured his own small hand against Grandpa's big one. "Just think," he said. "Once you were a small boy like me."

"Yes," said Grandpa. "And just think. Someday you will be a big old grandpa like I am."

The late afternoon sun made their shadows stretch out long and thin before them.

"Ever try to jump on your shadow?" asked
Grandpa.

"Easy," said William. He took a running leap.
He took three giant steps. He crouched down and
pounced like a cat on a mouse. But the shadow
boy always slid along the sidewalk ahead of him.

"I could never do it when I was your age,
either," said Grandpa. "My legs are longer now, of
course." Grandpa bent his long legs and jumped.

He ran and leaped until he was out of breath. "The old boy's still one jump ahead of me," he puffed. "I'll hold him down, William, and you jump on him for me."

Grandpa's house looked just as it always did. While Grandpa started supper, William put his duffel bag in the spare bedroom. Faded blue wallpaper poppies twined up the walls, just as William remembered. Through the open window he saw the lacy foliage of Grandma's jacaranda tree. Flat, round seedpods hung from the branches, looking William always thought, just like small brown turtles.

In the bathroom, Grandpa's shaving mug
smelled sweet and spicy. William held the shaving
brush under the faucet, stirred up a lather in the
mug, and painted a foamy white mustache under
his nose. He peered into the mirror on the
medicine cabinet and pulled at his eyebrows,
trying to make them curl up over his forehead the
way Grandpa's did. Then he rinsed his face and
went into the kitchen.

William peeled the papery skins off of a pair of onions. Grandpa chopped them and added them to the pot of chili bubbling away on the stove. "Onions make everything taste better," Grandpa said.

"Except ice cream," said William, and Grandpa laughed.

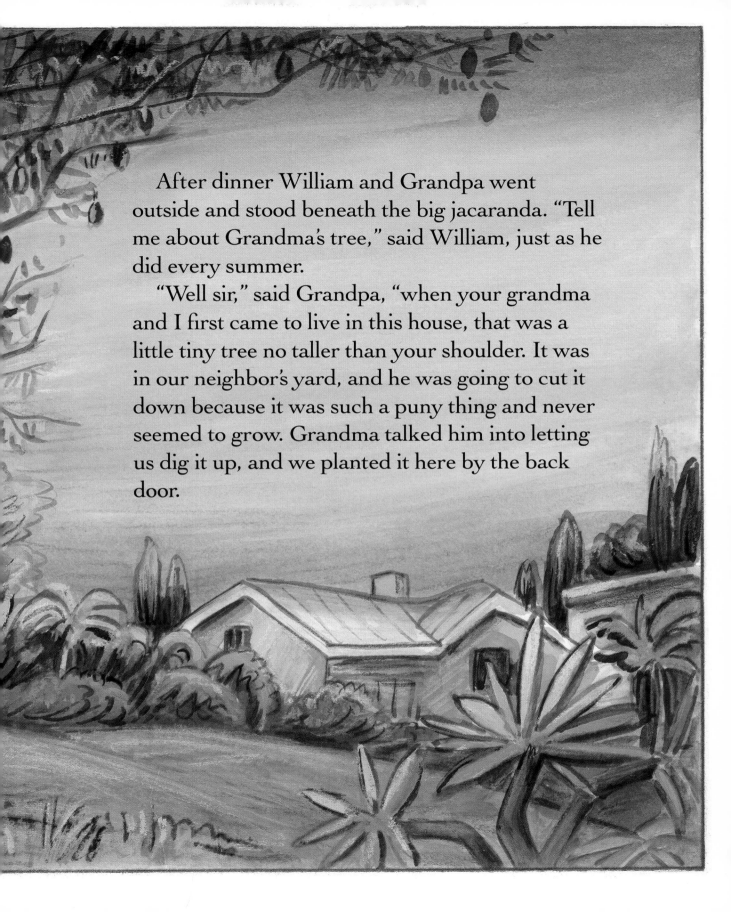

After dinner William and Grandpa went
outside and stood beneath the big jacaranda. "Tell
me about Grandma's tree," said William, just as he
did every summer.

"Well sir," said Grandpa, "when your grandma
and I first came to live in this house, that was a
little tiny tree no taller than your shoulder. It was
in our neighbor's yard, and he was going to cut it
down because it was such a puny thing and never
seemed to grow. Grandma talked him into letting
us dig it up, and we planted it here by the back
door.

"Grandma watered that tree and trimmed it and turned the earth beneath it. She took such good care of it that it began to grow. By the time our little boy was as big as you are, the tree was big enough for him to climb."

"That little boy was my daddy," said William.

"Yes," said Grandpa. He sat down in the yard swing, turning a seedpod over in his hand. "Grandma used to say these looked like turtles."

"She did?" said William. "That's what *I* always think, too!"

Grandpa's face wrinkled into a smile. "There's a lot of your grandma in you," he said.

"And some of you, too?" asked William.

Grandpa chuckled. "Yes, sir, some of me, too. And some of the great-great-grandmas and the great-great-great-grandpas we never knew."

Creak...creak...went the old swing as they
rocked back and forth. Darkness dropped gently
over the yard, and stars blinked on like tiny night-
lights, first one, then another.

"When I was a boy," said Grandpa, "I climbed to the top of the barn to look at the stars. A barn roof is a very good place for star watching."

William slipped his hand into Grandpa's. "Grandpa," he said, "would a *house* roof be a good place for star watching?"

Grandpa turned around in the swing and took a long look at the back of the house. "You never know till you try," he said.

They got a ladder from the garage and propped it against the side of the house. Hand over hand, and foot over foot, William climbed, with Grandpa right behind.

They lay back on shingles still warm from the afternoon sun. Hundreds and thousands and millions and billions of stars dotted the cold black bowl of the sky.

"Yes, sir," said Grandpa softly, "a house roof is a very good place for star watching."

"Grandpa," said William, "are they the same stars you saw when you were a boy?"

"The same stars," said Grandpa. "The very same."

"And I'll see the same stars when I am a big old grandpa like you?"

"Yes," said Grandpa. "You'll climb up on a roof with your grandson and tell him how you watched the very same stars with me."

William snuggled closer. "I wish we could stay up here all night."

"Me, too," said Grandpa. "There's only one trouble, though, with staying up on a roof all night. It was the same when I was a boy."

"What?" asked William.

Grandpa sighed. "There's no hot chocolate on a roof."

"Hot chocolate?" said William. "With marshmallows?"

Hand under hand, and foot under foot, they climbed down the ladder.

After William put on his pajamas, he watched Grandpa stir smooth, chocolaty syrup into a pan of foamy milk.

Then William climbed into bed and Grandpa sat beside him, each sipping from a steaming mug.

Grandpa told William about the little attic bedroom he had slept in as a boy. He told William about milking the cows every morning before the sun came up, and about filling the potbellied stove with wood he had chopped himself.

After a while Grandpa switched off the light
and took the two mugs into the kitchen.

William yawned and turned toward the window.
Through half-open eyes he saw the shadow of
the yard swing and the jacaranda tree, and beyond
them a sky full of stars. The same stars Grandpa
had seen as a boy. The same stars William would
see with his grandchildren. The same stars . . .

As his eyes closed, William heard Grandpa
rattling the dishes in the kitchen and singing softly,
"I went to the animal fair,
The birds and the beasts were there.
The big baboon
By the light of the moon
Was combing his auburn hair."